AJ WASHINGTON AND

THE BROTHERHOOD
OF THE ALL-SEEING EYE

AJ WASHINGTON AND
THE BROTHERHOOD
OF THE ALL-SEEING EYE

BOOK 1

ERIC BAKER

Primix Publishing
East Brunswick Office Evolution
1 Tower Center Boulevard, Ste 1510
East Brunswick, NJ 08816
www.primixpublishing.com
Phone: 1-800-538-5788

Published by Primix Publishing: 01/05/2026

ISBN: 979-8-89194-591-3(sc)
ISBN: 979-8-89194-592-0(e)

Library of Congress Control Number: 2026902015

CONTENTS

CHAPTER 1

MONSTERS IN THE CLOSET

He should have seen this coming. He should have known something like this would happen. Things were going way too good for him. These were the thoughts that were going through AJ Washington's mind as he sat on the hard, unforgiving pew at Tim, his foster father's funeral. He shifted his weight trying to get more comfortable, but there was no comfort to be had on the pew, just like there was no comfort to be had in his life.

AJ was a foster child, staying with Tim and Angela Jones. For the first time, he'd felt welcomed in a foster home. Tim and Angela had treated him like he was their own child, not just a way to get a paycheck from the government. "He and Tim had bonded almost immediately. Tim had played video games with him, helped him with his homework and done everything that a real dad would do with his son. And Angela had been the greatest foster mother ever. They watched tv together, laughed together and whenever the time called for it, she gave him a hug and a kiss to comfort him.

He had been with them for three months, longer than he had

stayed at any foster home since he'd been put into the foster system eight years ago. This brought up a memory he didn't need right now. His parents had disappeared when he was four years old, effectively abandoning him. He could only remember bits and pieces of them; sitting on his mom's lap while she tickled him, his father reading him a story.

This led to another unwanted memory, his last foster home. He had lived with Fred and Emily Anderson. Fred was an angry guy with a drinking problem. He was a nasty guy, and drinking just made him worse.

He would get drunk and beat Emily and AJ. When he was done, Emily, out of frustration, would turn on AJ and beat him some more. AJ had put up with this for two weeks before he ran away. Cindy, his social worker found him at the local soup kitchen three days later.

"Why did you run away this time AJ?" she asked him.

"I ran because both Fred and Emily were beating me! Do you want to see the bruises?" he asked Cindy.

And what would happen to him now that Tim was dead? Would Angela still want him? He almost wept at the idea of going back to foster care. He couldn't go to another foster home. Not now, after being with Tim and Angela. Would foster care let him stay even if she did want him? Angela was an attractive, Black woman in her late thirties, with long curly hair. But like many black women, she looked much younger than she was. She was also a licensed social worker who knew how to work the system, maybe she could arrange for him to stay with her. Suddenly, AJ's eyes glassed over, and his body stiffened. Angela who was sitting next to him felt his body tense and asked him if he was okay. But AJ couldn't respond because his consciousness had already left his body.

He found himself sitting alone in an Ancient Egyptian throne room. There were statues that honored past pharaohs and spiraled columns throughout the room. On the walls were murals of Egyptian gods doing various things. One that caught his eye was a mural of the goddess Maat. He didn't know how he knew who the goddess was, but he was positive it was the goddess Matt, goddess of justice. The throne he was sitting on was obviously for pharaoh. It was engraved with images of the gods, had wings carved into the back of it and was covered in gold. He looked around the throne room, one of the things that caught his eye were three large vases up against a wall. The vases were about three feet tall and decorated with images of the gods. They cast large shadows on the wall behind them. Oddly, one of the shadows began to move, the shadow took the form of a man and stepped away from the wall. The shadow/man turned to look at AJ and said,

"Pharaoh Ramses, you have united all of Egypt, if you ruled any longer you would unite the world. Lord Apep cannot allow this, you must die." And with that, the shadow demon pulled out a knife made of the same shadow substance he was and plunged it into AJ's heart. He screamed out for the god Horus as his body fell to the floor. Pharaoh's bodyguards came running in to find their ruler dying on the floor. By this point, the shadow demon had returned to looking like the shadow of one of the vases. The god Horus also came, but he was too late. Pharaoh Ramses was already dead. Horus wept to see such a good ruler killed in his prime.

The bodyguards asked AJ, "Who has done this to you, my lord?" All AJ could do was point at one of the vases before he died. AJ's consciousness immediately returned to his body. He felt like he was waking up from a bad dream, but he did not remember what had happened.

"Why are you staring at me?" he asked her moments later.

"Because you wouldn't answer me for the last minute or so, I thought you were having a mild seizure. What happened?" she replied. He had no recollection of anything that had happened, so he answered honestly,

I don't know."

"That's okay, we'll set you up with a doctor's appointment later."

"Okay," said AJ not really understanding what had just happened. Both AJ and Angela cried as the funeral ended and people walked up and gave their condolences. Angela drove AJ home after the funeral. Friends had brought food to the house for them to eat. The baked ham and potato salad were delicious, but AJ barely tasted it as he ate. The meal did not fill the hole in his heart. He missed Tim terribly.

The night after the funeral was the worst. That was when AJ first heard the monsters in his closet. AJ woke up to scratching noises coming from inside his closet. At first, he thought it might be rats, but then he heard the voices.

"We must kill the boy, or the master will punish us, yes we will kill the boy," they said in deep, guttural, not quite human voices. This prompted him to scream and run into Angela's room.

No parent likes to be woken up in the middle of the night by their child, but being woken up by a scream is one of the more frightening options. Angela popped up and shook her head to fully wake herself up. She got out of bed to go to him when he came running into her room.

The kid looked like a cartoon whirlwind of a person, arms flapping and yelling incoherently something about monsters trying to kill him. She inhaled deeply and placed her arms on his shoulders.

"AJ calm down. What happened?" She said, keeping her voice even and calm. In her experience, nothing was ever solved by panicking and she was hoping her composed demeanor would steady him. It only worked a little. AJ, eyes wide open with fear attempted to take a breath, but instead blurted out,

"There are monsters in my closet, and they want to kill me!"

Her first instinct was to comfort him, so she gave him a hug, and she was relieved that he accepted it, sinking into her arms and holding on to her like a lifeline. She let him cry, grateful that he felt comfortable showing his emotions to her. After all, they had not been family very long, and people had felt compelled to warn her that kids AJ's age were difficult and tended to hide their emotions.

The next thing that crossed her mind was that AJ was a bit old to believe in monsters. Of course, he had just lost the best foster father he had ever had, so PTSD was certainly a possibility. Throw in the fact that he'd been in foster care for most of his life and god only knew what had happened to him at his previous foster homes.

She decided that she would get AJ some help. Turned out she didn't have to. Help came for AJ all on its own.

The next day, the doorbell rang, and Angela answered the door. She opened the door and smiled widely at the visitor she saw. The visitor was a tall, muscular, Black man who obviously went out of his way to stay in shape. He wore wire rimmed glasses and had a neatly trimmed mustache and goatee.

"Hey Terry," she squealed giving him a hug. She was relieved to see him, and it showed by the smile on her face.

"It's good to see you too, Angie. I just thought it might be a good idea to check in on you and AJ.

Angela, obviously relieved to see him said, "I was just getting ready to call you. AJ thinks there are monsters in his closet or under his bed and they want to kill him. I thought it might just be PTSD from losing Tim so soon. But maybe you could talk to him, being a child psychologist and all.

Terry smiled and said, "Of course I'll talk to him. Is he home?"

"He's in his room," she turned and yelled back into the house, "AJ CAN YOU COME OUT HERE PLEASE? THERE'S SOMEONE HERE TO SEE YOU!" AJ trotted out and said,

Who would want to see me?" Terry smiled at AJ and said,

"Hi AJ, do you remember me?"

"Yeah, you're Terry. I remember when you, me and Tim played basketball at the Y. What are you doing here?" AJ asked.

"You have a good memory. I am Dr. Terrance Conners, child psychologist, known to you as Terry. I just dropped by to make sure things are going okay with you. Have you been having any problems lately?"

"Like what?" asked AJ tentatively.

"Well, Angela told me that you think that there are monsters in your closet that want to kill you," said Terry.

"Great, now she thinks I'm crazy!" replied AJ angrily. He was frustrated with Angela for betraying his trust, but mostly he was frustrated with himself for trusting her. But if he couldn't trust

Angela, who could he trust? That thought made him even more frustrated. That frustration was turning to anger.

"Angela does not think you're crazy," said Terry deliberately keeping his voice as calm as possible.

"Then why did she call you?" asked AJ, beginning to raise his voice.

"Calm down AJ. Please don't yell at me. Besides, she didn't call me. I just came by to check on you two. I know how hard it can be to lose a loved one. Since I'm here, why don't we talk for a little bit, because I think I might be able to help you." Said Terry.

"You can, how?" asked AJ looking at him with some hope, but not fully sure he could be trusted.

"With this," said Terry and showed AJ a gold necklace with a pendant on it.

"Hey, I know what that is!" Said AJ excitedly, "Tim told me about it. It's the Eye of Horus. Tim had a tattoo of it with an ankh on his forearm. At that moment, AJ noticed that Terry had the same tattoo that Tim had had.

"Were you and Tim in the same gang when you were younger?" he asked, "Is that why you have the same tattoo he had?"

Terry laughed and said, "Nothing so sinister, but we did belong to the same organization."

"What organization" asked AJ.

"I'll tell you more about it later," Terry answered mysteriously, "But for now let me explain how the amulet works. If the monsters come back, the Eye of "Horus is a powerful protection symbol, and it has the power to protect you. Legend has it, that this particular Eye of Horus was blessed by Horus himself. For it to work, you must truly believe in its power to protect you with all your heart," said Terry seriously.

Okay, so, all I have to do is believe that this amulet will protect me, and it will?" asked AJ.

"If you truly believe in its power, no monster in your closet can harm you. I give you my word." Said Terry.

Later that night, when he heard scratching on his closet door again. His heart beat with fear, but didn't scream or yell or do anything. It was when his closet door began to open that he stifled a scream. He focused on the amulet around his neck and thought to himself, "The Eye of Horus will protect me.

And then he got his first look at the monster as it came out of his closet. It looked like a boar that had learned to walk on two feet. It had long tusks growing out of its mouth, it wore armor, and carried a spear. AJ tried to scream, but no sound came out of his mouth. He wanted to run or hide, but he was frozen in fear. So, he did the only thing he could do. He concentrated on the amulet around his neck and thought, "The Eye of Horus will protect me" He thought it so hard that beads of sweat began to run down from his forehead. After a few seconds, the Eye of Horus responded. A blinding golden light burst forth from the eye and filled the room with golden light. When the light hit the monster, it growled in pain as it began to burn, the monster shrieked,

"The Eye of Horus! It burns!" And it was forced back into the closet where it had come from.

CHAPTER 2

BULLIES

AJ hummed happily to himself as he poured his favorite cinnamon cereal into a bowl for breakfast.

"Well, someone's in a good mood this morning," said Angela as she walked over to the coffee machine to brew a cup.

"No more monsters?" she asked carefully, hoping that he answered in the positive.

"No more monsters," AJ agreed, "Not only that they won't be coming back any time soon."

"Well, that's good news!" exclaimed Angela with a smile on her face.

"I gotta go or I'll miss the bus," said AJ as he grabbed his backpack, swung it over his shoulder and headed for the front door.

"Have a nice day, AJ," said Angela as he opened the front door.

"Thanks Angela, I'm sure I will. You do the same," replied AJ, patting the amulet around his neck. He walked out the door humming happily to himself. If only he knew what was coming, he would not have been in such a good mood. AJ walked to the bus stop. A group of kids were already there, talking to each other and laughing. He wasn't friends with any of them, so he stood by himself as far away from them as he could. Soon, the school bus arrived, and everyone got on for the ride to school.

AJ was the last to get on the bus. As he walked toward the back of the bus, the other kids scowled at him, letting him know that he was not welcome to sit with them. This was normal for AJ. He was new to this school and this neighborhood, so he didn't know anyone or have any friends. Having no friends made him a favorite target of bullies at whatever school he went to. Harriet Dubis Middle School was no different. As he made his way back to an empty seat at the back of the bus, someone stuck their leg out and tripped him, making him fall and drop his backpack.

"Have a nice trip?" Kyle Costello asked while sneering at him. AJ hurriedly picked up his backpack and sat down in the empty seat, his face burning with embarrassment. The other kids on the bus pointed at him and laughed. AJ did nothing except wish for the millionth time that he could turn into a big, green monster and smash his enemies. He hoped the Eye of Horus would help him again, but unfortunately, it only worked against real monsters, not human ones. The bus driver either didn't see what happened or didn't care because he pulled away from the curb as AJ was standing up and reaching for his backpack.

Kyle was such a stereotype of a bully that it wasn't even funny. First of all, he was the biggest kid in 8th grade. AJ suspected that this was because he had been held back a few times. This would also explain why he was the only kid in 8th grade that could grow a full beard. He was big and strong and enjoyed inflicting pain on others for no other reason than he could.

Finally, they arrived at school and the kids stopped laughing at him as they all got off the bus. AJ was last off the bus, under his breath he swore he would get revenge on all of them, someday, somehow. But deep down he knew he'd get no such revenge. AJ was a skinny, unpopular kid with no friends. Kyle on the other hand, had a slew of friends who followed him around to cheer him on when he was attacking his latest victim. The rest of the school day passed uneventfully. Nothing happened on the bus on the way home, apparently Kyle was in detention for bullying another student. AJ was in for a surprise when he got home. Terry was there waiting for him.

CHAPTER 3

A SURPRISE

"Hi Terry, how are you?" AJ greeted him.

"I'm fine, AJ. How was school today?"

"Okay, I guess," he replied timidly, but then quickly became more excited,

"The Eye of Horus worked! Just like you said it would!" he said happily, "How did you know it would work?"

Terry took a deep breath and began to explain. "Look AJ, Angie there's something you both need to know about. The other day, you noticed that Tim and I have the same tattoo. I told you that it was because we belonged to the same organization. It's time for you to learn more about that organization and what it means to you.

"Tim never told me about belonging to any organization and he told me he got that tattoo on a dare, when he was in college," interrupted Angela.

"He wouldn't have told you about the organization Angie," Terry proceeded cautiously, not wanting to hurt Angela's feelings. "He was trying to protect you, because some things once you know, you can't unknow. But now that Tim is gone and AJ is under attack, you both need to know the truth. No matter how bizarre or terrifying it may seem. You see AJ, it's no coincidence you ended up here. This is where you were meant to be. It's also not a coincidence that you started having problems with monsters after Tim died."

"What are you talking about?" Both AJ and Angela asked at the same time.

"Okay, this is going to be hard to explain and even harder to believe," Terry swallowed and started to explain. "First of all, the organization that Tim and I belonged to is called the Brotherhood of the All-Seeing Eye, BASE for short. BASE members are descendants of the ancient Egyptian gods. Tim, for example, was a descendant of Sekhmet, goddess of battle. A powerful warrior goddess. That's why his presence was enough to keep the monsters away. I am a descendant of Thoth, the god of writing."

"Wait, are you saying you think AJ's monsters are real!?!" Angela interrupted again.

"I'm afraid so, and I think AJ would agree with me. Did you see the monster in your closet last night?" he asked AJ.

"Definitely," replied AJ, a chill going down his spine just thinking about the monster that had come out of his closet, "How did you know the Eye of Horus would protect me and burn up the monster?" AJ asked.

"Let me tell you a story about ancient Egypt," said Terry instead of answering, "Thousands of years ago, when Egypt was at the height of all its glory, Lower Egypt and Upper Egypt were united into one kingdom by pharaoh Ramses. This united both the lands of Egypt and the people. This led to great prosperity for Egypt. Now, the main bad guy in Egyptian folklore is Apep, the god of chaos. He often takes the form of a giant snake. Now, when you're the god of chaos, countries and people being united kind of goes against everything you stand for. Apep worried that if Ramses stayed in power, he would unite all the people of the world. Uniting all the people in the world would mean there would be no chaos. Everything would be under control and when you're the god of chaos, you can't have that. So

Apep sent out one of his minions to assassinate Ramses. As Ramses died, he cried out for Horus to help him. Unfortunately, Horus got there too late. Ramses was already dead when he appeared at his side. Horus wept because he was sad to see such a good ruler die and asked his father, Osiris, god of the dead, if he would allow Ramses to return to the land of the living. Osiris refused, but seeing his son in such pain, he did allow for the pharaoh to be reincarnated every 100 generations to fulfill his destiny. The main job of the Brotherhood of the All-Seeing Eye is to find him before the forces of Apep do, so that we can explain all this and help him fulfill his destiny."

"Wait. And you think I'm this reincarnated pharaoh? That's crazy!" shouted AJ.

"You saw a demon with your own eyes, did you not?" asked Terry patiently, "And the fact that the Eye acted as it did in your presence proves that you are the reincarnation of Ramses. It would only protect you if you were him."

"I have a question," interjected Angela, "You said Tim was trying to protect me. Protect me from what?" she asked.

"From the truth. Once you know that demons are real and some conspiracies are true, you can start to see them everywhere. It can make you paranoid and make you lose touch with reality. Tim didn't want that for you. He loved you." Terry answered Angela as he turned toward AJ.

"And you need to be trained in the ways of ancient Egypt if you are going to survive." He said looking at AJ.

"What do you mean?" asked AJ.

"I mean you must be trained physically and metaphysically for the trials that are to come," Terry replied, "This attack was just the first of many to come. We must teach you how to defend yourself both physically and magically."

"How are we supposed to believe all of this Terry?" asked Angela, "I mean, Egyptian gods, pharaohs, demons. It all just sounds so crazy."

"I know how it sounds Angie and I know it's a lot to take in. But I believe it, Tim believed it and thousands of others believe it. And whether you want to believe it or not, these attacks are not going to stop until he fulfills his destiny." Terry responded.

"And what destiny is that? What is he supposed to do?" asked Angela.

"I'm sure I don't know. Only the journey is written, not the destination. And the first step on this journey starts with AJ beginning his training. Are you willing to start the training AJ?" Terry asked AJ.

"Um, I don't know," said AJ, not wanting to believe any of this.

"Perhaps I didn't make myself clear. The monster that came out of your closet was a low-level scout. It was sent to make sure you actually are the reincarnation. Now Apep knows for sure who you are. He will send stronger and stronger demons after you. The Eye can protect you from many of them, but the more training you have the better chance you have of surviving. So, I ask you again, are you willing to start the training?"

"Yes, I am," answered AJ realizing he didn't really have a choice.

"Good, training starts on Saturday, I'll pick you up at 10:00.

CHAPTER 4

THE TRAINING BEGINS

Saturday morning at 5:00 AJ was wide awake, not with fear but with excitement. Today his training would begin, and he had no idea what that would entail. Would he learn martial arts, like kung-fu? Or even cooler would he learn magic? As excited as he was, he was also worried. What if he wasn't any good? What if he was so bad that he failed the training? What would happen to him then? Would Angela send him back to foster care? All these questions ran through his head as he lay in bed waiting for the day to start.

After tossing and turning for hours trying uselessly to get to sleep. AJ got out of bed at 9:00 to get dressed. After he was dressed, he went to the kitchen to get some cereal for breakfast. He ate his bowl of cereal at the kitchen table and just as he finished the doorbell rang. He walked quickly to the door, trying not to explode with excitement. He opened the door and there stood Terry in a sweatsuit.

"Are you going to teach me martial arts?" AJ blurted out excitedly.

"No, you'll be learning to protect yourself physically from someone else. I'm here to teach you about the mystical arts of ancient Egypt.

Come on, let's go to my office." AJ climbed into Terry's car and off they went.

"What are you going to teach me?" asked AJ after they were both in the car.

"I'm going to teach you about Egyptian history and how you can use Egyptian magic to your advantage," Terry answered.

"You're going to teach me to use magic?" asked AJ intrigued.

"Ancient Egyptian history and Egyptian magic go hand in hand. You can't learn one without learning the other." Replied Terry, "There's something else I wanted to talk to you about. You seem to think your parents abandoned you and I don't think that's true. It's much more likely that they were kidnapped by the forces of Apep." Said Terry.

"Why would Apep want to kidnap my parents?" asked AJ.

"So he could use them to control and manipulate you. I'll explain all of this later," he said hurriedly as they arrived at his office. As they were walking up the steps to Terry's office, AJ asked another question.

"If Apep wants me dead, why didn't he just kill me when I was a baby, instead of kidnapping my parents?"

"That is a good question. From what we know, the god Horus was so distraught when Ramses died that he begged his father, Osiris, to allow Ramses to return to the world of the living. Osiris refused but feeling sorry for his son, did allow for Ramses to be reincarnated every hundred generations. You are the latest reincarnation. Osiris also put a blessing on this reincarnation so that no evil could harm him until he reached the Age of Ascension,"

"What's the Age of Ascension?" interrupted AJ.

"The Age of Ascension is the age when a boy could officially become pharaoh, 12. That's why demons have started attacking you now. You've reached the Age of Ascension. Apep can send his agents to kill you now. That's why you must learn to defend yourself. Tim was a descendant of Sekhmet, goddess of war and battle. So, his presence was powerful enough to keep the demons at bay. But when he was murdered, it became open season on you." Said Terry.

"What do you mean murdered? I thought he was killed during a mugging attempt?" Said AJ.

"Tim was not mugged. He was murdered," said Terry wistfully, "He was killed by the agents of Apep. At least that's what we believe at BASE. Tim getting mugged never made any sense. The man was 6'2" 240 pounds of muscle. He was a former Green Beret, so he knew how to handle himself in a fight. He also wasn't stupid. If someone pulled a gun on him, he would have given up his wallet without a fight. No, he wasn't mugged, he was murdered."

"But why??" asked AJ

"As I told you, his mere presence was enough to keep the demons away. They needed him out of the way to get to you." Said Terry.

"So, you're saying Tim died because of me?" asked AJ suddenly feeling guilty.

"No, don't think that way. Tim died fighting for a cause he believed in. His death is not your fault." Said Terry. "Anyway, back to your training. Magic is mostly about asking the right god for a favor. And doing it in the right way. The last thing you want to do is offend a god, trust me. So, here is a list of gods you might be calling on. Your homework is to memorize each god and their domain. I should also mention that your homework is due tomorrow."

"Wait a minute. You expect me to memorize all these gods' names and their domains by tomorrow? How am I supposed to do that?" AJ whined.

"I suggest you make flash cards. Besides, there are only about twelve gods there and you don't have to learn about Sobek. He is the crocodile god and the last thing we need to throw into this mix is crocodiles. I suggest you get to work on those flash cards. Ask Angela to help you. I'm sure she'd be glad to help. Hey, I never said training would be fun or easy, but it just might save your life."

Terry dropped AJ off at home, where AJ immediately began making flash cards of the Egyptian gods. He asked Angela to help him, and before he knew it, he had memorized the names of the gods and their domains. When Angela asked him, "Who is the god of the dead?" The answer immediately popped into his head.

"Osiris," he answered without really thinking about it. The next morning, at exactly 10:00 the doorbell rang, and it was Terry.

"Did you finish your homework?" he asked AJ.

"Yeah, it was way easier than I thought it would be," said AJ.

"Yes, I thought it might be. You see, I'm not asking you to learn anything new. I'm just asking you to remember what you already know. And another thing, Angie, AJ, I need you both to pay attention to this. The mild seizure that AJ had at the funeral. I don't think it was a seizure at all. I think you're remembering when you were pharaoh."

"Then why didn't I remember what happened?" asked AJ.

"Because technically, it's not your memory. It's from a different life. I think the more training you get, the less it will happen. And speaking of training, next week you start your physical training."

"What kind of physical training?" asked AJ. He was both excited and worried at the same time. He was excited to be taught self defense by an MMA champion. He was worried that he wouldn't be any good.

"I'm sure I don't know, but your teacher is an MMA champion."

"Do I get to learn Mixed Martial Arts? That is so cool!" exclaimed AJ.

"It's not his job to be cool," said Terry, "It's his job to keep you alive! Now that you've memorized the gods and their domains, there are some hieroglyphs you need to learn. You may not always have time to write down a spell, but a spell is strongest when it is both written and spoken out loud. It is even more powerful when it is written in hieroglyphs. Also practice writing hieroglyphs. "That's your homework, and it's due the day after tomorrow.

"Hieroglyphs," AJ moaned, "I hope they come as easy as the gods' names did."

"They should, again, you're just remembering what you already know." Said Terry, "Before I forget, your physical training instructor is named Billy Olson. As I told you he is an MMA champion, and he will meet you at the Y on Saturday. I will pick you up and introduce the two of you. As AJ got out of the car, he noticed a movement out of the corner of his eye and saw a black cat walking by a tree in his front yard. The cat turned and stared at him for a moment and then walked away. He didn't recognize the cat, so he thought nothing of it."

"Your first meeting with Billy at 1:00. I will pick you up." Before he drove away, he said,

"Good luck with your physical training. Billy Olson might not be what you expect. I'll see you next week and work on those hieroglyphs!" He said as he drove away.

The rest of the week passed without any more demon attacks. Thanks to the Eye of Horus that hung around his neck at all times. Saturday came and Terry came to pick him up. They went to the Y and AJ finally met Billy Olson. Terry had not been joking when he said that Billy might not be what he expected. First of all, he was short. I mean really short, like 5 foot 5 inches. Second, he was a white guy, with long hair and a mustache and beard. He certainly did not look like AJ thought an MMA champion should look. A look of surprise fluttered across his face as he tried to hide his surprise and disappointment.

Billy noticed this. "You don't think I look like an MMA champion, do you?" Billy asked him.

"Well, um," AJ stuttered in response.

"Looks can be deceiving," said Billy and in the blink of an eye his fist was just mere inches from AJ's face. Suddenly, Billy unleashed a flurry of punches, each landing inches from AJ's face. The punches came so quickly that AJ could barely see them, and then he stopped.

"Wow!" AJ said in awe, "I've never seen anyone punch so fast."

"This type of speed comes with time, training and practice. I have reserved a room for us train let's go." And so, AJ's physical training began.

"Well, ancient Egyptians were known for their stick fighting ability and their grappling techniques. So, let's start there. Billy took a Bo-staff out of his bag and tossed it to AJ. AJ easily caught it and began to twist it around. Billy said,

"Look, you're natural," and then began to show AJ how to use the Bo staff in a fight. After a few weeks of training, AJ was very good with a Bo-staff and Billy was impressed.

"Your stick fighting has improved faster than I thought it would. You must have been a stick fighter when you were pharaoh. You don't need any more training in stick fighting. In fact, I have a gift for you." He reached into his bag and pulled out a staff made from gold. "Until you fulfill your destiny, demons are going to be attacking you day and night. You're going to need a weapon to defend yourself. May I present to you the staff of Ramses the Great. This is a very special Bo-staff. I realize you can't walk around with a full-size Bo staff without getting some unwanted attention. So, he yelled, "Baka!" and the staff shrunk down to the size of a number 2 pencil. AJ stared in awe at Billy and asked,

"How did you do that?"

"Oh, the staff is magical. I probably should have mentioned that first. Also, the staff is made of Pharaoh's gold." Said Billy.

"What's Pharaoh's Gold?" asked AJ still looking at Billy in awe.

"The legend goes that Pharaoh's Gold was given to Ramses by Ra himself to fashion weapons that could dispel demons. In other words, it's like Kryptonite for demons. To bring it back to its regular size just say Baka! Say the same thing to shrink it back down again" Said Billy AJ took the Bo-staff and said, "Baka!" The staff grew back to its regular size. He began to twist it and maneuver it in his hands. Although it was made of gold, it was extremely light and easy to maneuver. AJ felt like the staff had been made especially for him.

"Now we start the MMA training," said Billy, "Let's start with punching." He pulled out some pads that covered his hands and told AJ to punch the pads. AJ tapped the pads lightly.

"Harder!" shouted Billy, "I want maximum effort!" AJ began punching the pads with more effort. "That's better. Now, when you punch, you need to put your whole body behind it and focus all your power into your punch." For the next hour AJ practiced his punches, by punching Billy. After a week, Billy said,

"Your punches are becoming more powerful; I think I'm going to need thicker padding." Days turned into weeks, and weeks turned into months of AJ training with Billy and Terry. His fighting skills improved dramatically while training with Billy. His punches were powerful and fast and so were his kicks. This along with learning Egyptian history and magic from Terry substantially boosted AJ's self-esteem.

CHAPTER 5

THE PRINCIPAL

He was just starting to believe in himself when it happened. He was shooting hoops by himself at brunch, when someone pushed him from behind and took the basketball from him. Of course, it was Kyle. AJ picked himself up from the ground, mumbling under his breath. He realized he was praying to the Egyptian god of battle to help him in the upcoming fight.

"How dare you put me your hands on me, you oaf?" AJ wondered who could be talking to Kyle like this and was shocked when he realized the words had come out of his own mouth. He wasn't sure who was more surprised, him or Kyle. Kyle's surprise and confusion wore off quickly and he did what all bullies do. He tried to punch AJ. His face was contorted with rage as he threw the first punch.

AJ, who had been waiting for this, felt like time slowed down. Kyle's fist seemed to approach him in slow motion. AJ easily dodged Kyle's fist while simultaneously kicking him in the spleen, knowing this would bring his enemy to his knees. As Kyle tried to get back up, AJ unleashed a flurry of blows to finish him off. The kids around them who had been chanting, "Fight, Fight, Fight," stopped chanting out of shock. Their champion had been beaten.

Suddenly, someone grabbed him by the back of his shirt. He turned to see Mr. Towers, the yard duty, grabbing him and Kyle. "Come on boys, off to the principal with both of you," he said. AJ was happy to see that Kyle had a bloody nose and was struggling to get to his feet. They were both taken to the principal's office. Dr. Ben Richardson was written on the principal's door. Mr. Towers knocked on the door and Principal Richardson's voice boomed from behind the door,

"Come in"

"I caught these two fighting Dr. Richardson," said Mr. Towers. The principal put his hands in his lap and calmly looked at the two boys. Mr. Towers left the room without another word. The principal sighed and said,

"Kyle, why don't you go back to class, Alexander and I have some things to discuss." AJ was outraged! Why did Kyle get to go back to class when he was the one who started everything? And why was he being forced to stay in this office just for defending himself? He was so mad he could barely speak! "How come...? Why am I...?" AJ tried to ask the principal questions, but his words kept getting tripped up by his anger.

"Do you really think I don't know who you are?" he asked in a voice too deep to be human. As he looked at AJ from behind his desk, he smiled and evil smile and his eyes began to emit a red glow. AJ could feel the Eye of Horus spreading warmth throughout his body, until the room shone with light. But the light was not coming from the Eye, it was coming from AJ himself.

Then there was a knock on the door and in walked Jamal Walker. Jamal and AJ were in the same English class. Jamal was tall, slim, and athletically built. He was also captain of the basketball team, and he was popular. He walked in to see AJ glowing with light and the principal's eyes emitting an ungodly red glow.

This is not over Alexander!" exclaimed Dr. Richardson, but the red glow faded from his eyes until they were their usual brown color. A puff of smoke came out of his mouth, and he coughed up a slug the size of a ping pong ball. The slug thing hit the floor and disappeared in a puff of smoke.

AJ had stopped glowing by this point, and the principal looked like he was waking up from a nightmare.

"What happened? Where am I? AJ, Jamal, what are you doing here?" he asked, obviously confused.

"I just came to get AJ," said Jamal, looking as confused as the principal did.

"Fine, take him and go back to class. Wait a minute! AJ what are you doing in here?"

"You said you wanted to talk to me." Replied AJ, "Can I go back to class now?"

"Yes, yes, both of you go back to class" he said gruffly. Both boys nearly tripped over themselves trying to get out of the principal's office. After they were safely out of Dr. Richardson's office, Jamal turned to AJ and said, "What just happened? Tell me you saw that slug thing come out of his mouth and I'm not just trippin' This is crazy, man. By the way, I saw you fight with Kyle. That was a serious beatdown you put on him. I don't think he'll be messing with you again."

"I'm not sure what just happened," said AJ "but I think I know who to ask to find out. After I find out what happened back there, I'll explain it to you, okay."

"Okay. You're pretty cool AJ. We should hang out at lunch," said Jamal. And just like that AJ made his first friend at Harriet Dubois Middle School.

CHAPTER 6

A NEW FRIEND

As AJ and Jamal walked back to class together, they talked about what had just happened.

"Do you think the principal was possessed by an alien?" Jamal asked AJ.

"I don't know," replied AJ, "but he was definitely possessed by something."

"Did you see that slug thing come out of his mouth?" asked Jamal. "Shouldn't we tell someone? I mean if people are getting possessed by aliens, we should probably tell someone right?

"Yeah, but who? Who would believe us? I don't think the principal even knows that he was possessed," replied AJ.

"I know my parents would think I was either crazy or lying, if I told them that the principal had been possessed by an alien," said Jamal

"I think I might know someone who would believe us," said AJ, thinking of Terry.

"We'd better get back to class before Ms. Henderson sends out a search party for us" They left the bewildered principal behind and walked back to class.

"Who do you know that would believe something like this?" asked Jamal.

"My therapist," answered AJ.

"Oh great, you're in therapy." Said Jamal, "Well if your therapist doesn't already think you're crazy, he will if you tell him about this!"

"I don't think so, he's not like that. I think he'll believe us," AJ said as they arrived at English class.

"Hello AJ, Jamal how nice of the principal to let you come back to class," Said Ms. Henderson sarcastically. Both boys went to their desks.

"AJ can you please come up here. You weren't here when I handed back last week's test." AJ walked up to the teacher's desk wondering how bad he had done on the test. She handed him his test and it had an A- written across the top. He looked at the grade again to make sure he'd seen it correctly.

"Are you okay?" she asked him, quietly under her breath. She rolled up her sleeve to reveal a tattoo of an ankh and the Eye of Horus intertwined, just like Terry's.

"Terry told me to keep an eye on you. I thought it was weird that the principal let Kyle go back to class but held you in his office. That's why I sent Jamal to get you."

"Good thing you did. I think he was possessed by a demon." He told her what had happened in the principal's office.

"I should have guessed. Ben being such a corrupt person. It was inevitable that he would allow himself to be possessed by an Asfet." She said.

"What is an Asfet?" asked AJ.

I'll explain later," answered Ms. Henderson, "Right now, you need to get back to your desk before the other students start wondering what we're talking about." AJ went back to his desk and sat down. Soon the bell rang, and everybody got up to go to lunch. AJ was looking for Jamal, when Ms. Henderson called him.

"AJ, can I see you for a moment please?" AJ turned around and walked back to the front of the classroom.

"Yes, Ms. Henderson?"

"I just wanted to finish our conversation from earlier. An Asfet is a demon that can possess people who are willing to sell their body and soul for something they want. You'd be surprised how many people are willing to sell their soul for things like fame and fortune. Anyway, you should tell Terry about the attack." AJ nodded thoughtfully and thanked her for the information and the advice and left the classroom to catch up with the other students. Jamal caught up to him in the hallway.

"What did Ms. Henderson want with you?" he asked AJ.

"She just wanted to talk to me about my test," said AJ. He wasn't willing to tell Jamal the truth that he was a reincarnated pharaoh and a demon had possessed their principal to try and kill him. That sounded even crazier than aliens possessing people. And he didn't want to scare off his only friend. They chatted about aliens possessing people as they walked to the school cafeteria.

"I saw your fight with Kyle, those were some wicked moves you used. Do you study martial arts?

"Just a little MMA," AJ responded.

"That's cool. I study Kung-Fu. You should come over to my house after school and maybe we could teach each other some moves." Said Jamal.

"That sounds cool. Where do you live?" AJ asked. Just then, an attractive Black girl came up to their table and sat next to Jamal and said,

Hey Jamal, who's your friend?" smiling at AJ.

Jamal rolled his eyes and said,

"Divia this is AJ. AJ this is my sister Divia." AJ's heart skipped a beat as he shook her hand. He had never seen such a beautiful girl. He tried to think of something witty to say, but all he could manage was "Hi". Divia smiled at him and said,

"I'll see you around AJ." Then she got up and left.

"Sorry about that, she's my little sister what are you going to do?" he asked rolling his eyes. "By the way, those were some wicked moves you used on Kyle, do you study martial arts?"

"Just a little MMA," replied AJ.

"That's cool. I study Kung-Fu. You should come over to my house after school and we could teach each other some moves." Said Jamal.

"Sounds cool, where do you live?" asked AJ.

"I live on Hardisty Way, over by the old grocery store. Where do you live?" Jamal replied.

"I actually live kind of close to you. I live on Angora Place, over by the old grocery store. We're practically neighbors" said AJ excitedly.

"Okay, how about this, I've got some stuff to do after school today, but after that I'm free. Can you come over around 4:30 today?" asked Jamal.

"Yeah, sure I can. What's your address?" asked AJ.

"1426 Hardisty Way," said Jamal. AJ put his address in his phone, and they began to eat lunch and talk. They talked about martial arts, video games and their favorite basketball players. But mostly they talked about whether aliens were invading earth and possessing people. The bell rang and they said goodbye and went back to their classes.

Finally, the last bell rang, and it was time to go home. They both got on the school bus, and for the first time AJ had a friend to sit with on the bus. When AJ's stop came, he got up to leave, said goodbye to Jamal, with a promise of coming over to see him later.

CHAPTER 7

BASTET

He was in for a surprise when he got home. Angela greeted him at the front door and said, "You know what, AJ? You have a lot on your plate, and I think I know what might make things a little easier for you. I think you need a pet. After dinner, we'll go down to the pound and you can pick out any pet you like."

"That sounds great, but can we do it tomorrow? I just made a new friend and I'm supposed to be at his house at 4:30."

"We can just do it now and you'll have plenty of time to see your new friend. Why don't you go get in the car and we'll go get you a new pet."

"Okay," said AJ as he headed out the door toward the car. As they drove to the pound Angela said,

"I know things have been difficult for you lately; Having Tim die, dealing with monsters and all that comes with that. I just thought having a pet might make you feel more grounded, you know, more normal. Would you like a dog or a cat?" asked Angela.

"I don't know. I've never had a pet before," answered AJ as

they arrived at the pound. They walked into the pound and were immediately inundated with the sounds of barking and meowing. They were greeted by a worker who told them to feel free to walk around and get a better look at the animals. They looked at the dogs first. There were so many different dogs, in so many different emotional states. He saw an angry looking Chihuahua, and a pit bull that looked scared for his life. But none of these seemed right for him, so he moved on to the cats. Immediately, AJ saw the cat he had seen outside their house. The cat stared straight at him, as if daring him to adopt her. AJ immediately knew that this was the pet for him.

"That black cat right there, I want her," said AJ to Angela. She motioned for a worker to release the cat. As the worker opened the cage door, the cat raced out of the cage and jumped into AJ's arms.

"Well, she appears to like you too," said Angela, "What are you going to name it?" AJ thought about it for a moment, when suddenly a female voice popped into his head and said, "Bastet, my name is Bastet!"

After he got over the initial shock of hearing a voice in his head, AJ said, "Bastet, her name is Bastet."

"That's an interesting name," said Angela, "How do you know it's a female?"

Y "I don't know. I just do." Answered AJ. The worker confirmed that the cat was indeed female and had not been spayed. Angela paid the worker a fee for the cat and it was put into a crate for them to take home. They left the city pound and stopped at a pet store on the way home and bought supplies for the cat; some cat food, a few toys and a flea collar. When they got home, AJ took the cat into his room and spoke to her.

"Are you the goddess Bastet?" he asked her, feeling stupid talking to a cat. At first, the cat just stared at him, then she began licking herself. Suddenly there was a blinding light and the cat transformed into a beautiful African woman. With skin the color of a roasted coffee bean, dark almond shaped eyes and long black hair that rolled down her back.

"Of course I am," she said. AJ looked at her in awe, speechless.

It was just too much for his brain to process, and AJ fainted. He regained consciousness a moment later. He opened his eyes to find his cat staring at him.

"Bastet?" he asked cautiously. The cat merely yawned in response. "It must have been my imagination," he thought to himself. He picked himself up off the floor and left the room. He told Angela he was going to his new friend Jamal's house. She asked him if he needed a ride, but AJ decided to walk to get the cobwebs out of his head after what happened with Bastet. It took AJ ten minutes to walk to Jamal's house. He rang the doorbell and waited. Soon, the door was answered by Jamal's sister, Divia.

"Hey AJ, what are you doing here?" she asked, smiling at him.

"I'm here to see Jamal, is he here?" he replied.

"Sure, I'll get him for you," she said, sounding a little disappointed. Soon Jamal appeared at the door and said,

"Hey man, glad you could make it. Come on in, I'll show you my room." They both walked into the house. Jamal's room was at the back of the house on the right. AJ walked in and looked around. The walls were covered with posters of Bruce Lee performing various martial arts moves. Scattered among the Bruce Lee posters were posters of various NBA players.

"Do you want to play basketball or work on some martial arts moves?" Jamal asked AJ.""

"Let's shoot some hoops," replied AJ. Jamal grabbed a basketball out of his closet. They went to the hoop that was right outside Jamal's house and played Horse. Then they played 21. They were pretty evenly matched on the basketball court and Jamal said,

"You're pretty good AJ. You should try out for the basketball team next year." After playing basketball for about a half an hour, they went into Jamal's garage to practice martial arts. AJ was showing Jamal how to do a jumping side kick, when Divia walked in and said,

"Jamal, mama says dinner will be ready soon, so get cleaned up. She also said that AJ can stay for dinner if he wants to."

"I would love to stay for dinner, I'm starving." Said AJ. The two boys went to the bathroom and washed their hands and faces, and came into the kitchen for dinner. A large bowl of spaghetti and meatballs was in the middle of the kitchen table. Next to it was a salad and a loaf of garlic bread. AJ's mouth watered at the smell of the garlic bread. Divia and Jamal's mom were already seated at the table. The boys sat down and began to heap food on their plates.

"Hello AJ, my name is Melissa, and I'm Jamal's mom," Jamal's mom introduced herself.

"Hello ma'am, nice to meet you. Thank you for having me for dinner." Said AJ between bites of garlic bread. After dinner, while helping wash dishes, AJ looked outside and saw how dark it was getting.

"Oh, it's getting late, I better get home," said AJ. He said goodbye to Jamal and his family and started walking home. As soon as he got home, he called Terry to tell him about what happened at school.

"So, you say you and Jamal saw this slug like creature come out of your principal's mouth? That's odd, because only descendants of Egyptian gods can see demons. So, he is either the descendant of an Egyptian god, or he is someone very special." Said Terry.

"One other thing, I got a new cat and I think she is the goddess Bastet," said Terry trying to sound calm and rational and not crazy. He explained to Terry about hearing the goddess's voice in his mind, and how she transformed from a cat to a woman and how he fainted. AJ was embarrassed about fainting, but he told the truth about what happened.

"Well, she was speaking directly to your mind. That can be unnerving, and then transforming in front of you, without warning. I can see why you fainted." Said Terry, noticing that AJ was embarrassed.

"When I woke up, I tried talking to her, but she didn't say anything. I wasn't sure if my mind was just playing tricks on me," AJ concluded.

"It was not your imagination playing tricks on you and you are not losing your mind," said Terry confidently, "I believe that your cat is the goddess Bastet. So, the first thing to do is go back and talk to her. Find out why she is here. If she transforms again, I don't think you'll faint, because you've experienced it before." Said Terry. AJ thanked Terry for the advice and went home. He went to his room, where the cat was lying on his bed, apparently waiting for him.

"Okay, let's try this again. Are you the goddess Bastet?" he asked. A voice responded in his mind,

"Why do you ask questions that you already know the answers to?"

"Okay, so you are the goddess Bastet, what do you want with me? Once again, the cat transformed into a woman. This time AJ was ready for it and didn't even bat an eye. The goddess looked at AJ intently for a moment and then finally she spoke.

"For centuries the gods lain dormant, waiting for your return, and in that time, Apep has spread chaos and corruption across the land. But now, you have returned,

and the gods have wakened! I am here to help you fulfill your destiny."

"But I don't even know what my destiny is. How am I supposed to fulfill my destiny if I don't know what it is?" asked AJ.

"Then we will find out what your destiny is together, you and your trusty cat," replied Bastet morphing back into a cat.

CHAPTER 8

THE GREAT SPHINX

"First of all, how am I supposed to find out what my destiny is?" asked AJ, as they both sat on his bed, her in cat form. Her voice responded in his mind,

"In my day, when there was an important question one needed answered, there was only one oracle to see."

"And who was that?" asked AJ.

"The Great Sphinx knows the answer to every question," replied Bastet.

"The Great Sphinx!" AJ yelled in surprise. "How am I supposed to see the Great Sphinx? The last time I checked, the Great Sphinx was in Egypt, right?"

"That is correct."

"As a goddess you may be able to go and do whatever you want. But I'm a 12-year-old with no money. How am I supposed to get to Egypt?" said AJ growing angrier with each word.

"I'm sure an opportunity will present itself and remember AJ, you are Pharaoh Ramses, Egypt is within you." Said Bastet mysteriously, and then being a cat, she went to sleep and with that the conversation ended.

Later, AJ called Terry to tell him about his conversation with Bastet. As he explained what she had said, Terry nodded and stroked his goatee.

"Have you been practicing your meditation and controlling your dreams?" he asked AJ

"Not really," AJ admitted timidly.

"Well, tonight is a great night to start doing it again. Before you go to bed tonight, I want you to meditate for one hour and try to control your dreams. Also, I would like to meet your friend Jamal, would it be okay if I came to your house to meet him?" Terry asked.

"Okay," said AJ, "I'll practice meditating and controlling my dreams tonight and I'll tell Jamal you want to meet him," AJ answered.

"Great, I look forward to meeting him and seeing you again. Goodbye AJ, I'll call you tomorrow," said Terry and hung up.

For the first time in weeks, AJ meditated. He tried to concentrate on one thing and one thing only. First, he decided to try and concentrate on Divia. He thought about her face with her sparkling green eyes, her pouty mouth and high cheekbones. He thought about how good she looked at school today in blue jeans and a green tank top that matched her eyes. He thought about how much he wanted to kiss her. That last thought came as a bit of a shock to AJ. Divia was pretty and all, but she was his best friend's sister. More honestly, she was his only friend's sister. Focusing on Divia was a bad idea, it led to way too many other thoughts. So, he tried to concentrate on the Great Sphinx. He focused on how much he needed to speak to her. He managed to completely focus on his need to speak with the Great Sphinx and then the strangest thing happened. He found himself walking down a dark hallway. As he walked forward, torches on the wall lit up as he passed them. AJ was scared, but for some reason he knew he had to keep walking forward. After about 50 feet, the hallway ended and opened into a room. At the end of the room was a giant pedestal. Sitting on the pedestal was the Great Sphinx herself.

"Approach and ask Alexander James Washington," boomed a

voice that seemed to come from everywhere. AJ approached the Sphinx and kneeled before her and asked,

"Oh, Great Sphinx, what is my destiny?"

"It is your destiny to find those whom you have lost." The Sphinx answered and then the lights went out, the flames in the torches flickered and went out and AJ woke up in his bed.

"Bastet, where are you?" he said into the seemingly empty room.

"I am right here," said who was lying on the floor next to AJ's bed in cat form.

"I just had a dream; the Great Sphinx was there. I know my destiny!" said AJ excitedly.

"I know, I was the one controlling your dream. If you had your way, you would have dreamt about that girl," said Bastet, mid-yawn.

The Sphinx said that it is my destiny to find those whom I have lost. I think that means my parents. But how do I find them?" he asked Bastet.

"We should sleep now, tomorrow, tomorrow I will help you find your parents and fulfill your destiny,' said Bastet, as she fell asleep. Even as excited as he was AJ soon fell asleep as well.

The next morning, AJ called Terry to tell him what he had learned. "Hey AJ, what's up?" said Terry as he answered his phone.

"Terry, you won't believe what happened!" Said AJ excitedly.

"You'd be surprised by what I would believe, but please, tell me what happened," Terry responded.

"My cat is the goddess Bastet and we discovered what my destiny is," AJ was so excited, all the words tumbled out of his mouth all at once.

"That's great, how did you do it?" asked Terry. AJ told him about his dream and meeting the Sphinx and her telling him his destiny.

"You got to meet the Great Sphinx and she actually spoke to you?" asked Terry in awe.

"Yeah, but like I said it was just a dream," answered AJ.

"No, it wasn't. Bastet used your dream to transport your consciousness to Egypt. The

"But, no, it was just a dream. I woke up in my bed," argued AJ..

"Of course you did, she only needed your consciousness, not your physical body," said Terry calmly.

"How do you know?" asked AJ

"Because the great Sphinx does not visit anyone in their dreams, not even pharaoh.   If one wants the counsel of the Sphinx, one must go to see it in Egypt." Answered Terry, once again in a calm voice. "By the way, what did the Sphinx say to you?"

"She said my destiny is to find those whom I have lost. I think she meant my parents. Do you know where Apep is holding my parents?" Asked AJ

"I'm afraid I don't. But I'll do some research and see if I can find out." Said Terry. The next day was Saturday and AJ was eating breakfast with Angela. She had made pancakes for the two of them. He had told her how his cat was the Egyptian goddess Bastet and how he had found out his destiny. Angela thought about it for a minute and said,

"Well, I'm glad you have a god on your side." Then she changed the subject, " I've noticed you spending a lot of time at Jamal's house lately. It's great that you have a new friend, does he know about you?" she asked.

"What do you mean?" asked AJ innocently.

"You know what I mean. Does he know about the monsters in your closet and who you really are?" She pressed.

"Jamal is the only friend I've got. If I tell him all that stuff, he'll think I'm crazy and never talk to me again." Said AJ.

"Well, a demon attacked you in front of him already, he could have been hurt. Fortunately, neither of you were. Doesn't he deserve to know the truth? If you don't want to do it, maybe Terry could. It might sound more believable coming from an adult," she said.

"You're right. Jamal is a good friend, and he deserves to know the truth. Terry has been wanting to meet him anyway, so I'll let him explain everything." Said AJ. Later that day, AJ called up Jamal.

"Hey man, do you want to come over and practice some Kung-Fu moves?" AJ asked Jamal.

"Sounds good, I'll be over in about an hour," replied Jamal. An hour later, they were practicing martial arts in AJ's garage. After that, they decided to relax and watch some TV. Angela had just brought them some lemonade, when the doorbell rang. AJ opened the front door and Terry was standing there. AJ ushered him into the house. He brought Terry into the den, where he and Jamal were watching TV.

"Hey Jamal, remember when I told you about my therapist? Well, this is him, his name is Terry," said AJ to Jamal.

"Hello Jamal, pleased to meet you," said Terry extending a hand towards him. Jamal looked at him skeptically and said,

"I'm not crazy and I don't need therapy."

"I agree with you," said Terry, "I don't think you're crazy, nor do I think you need therapy. But there is that thing about aliens possessing people, isn't there? Wouldn't you like to know what that thing really was?"

"You know what it was?" asked Jamal with awe.

"Yes, I believe I do. But just to be clear, did you actually see the creature that came out of your principal?" asked Terry.

"Yeah, it looked like a big slug" Answered Jamal.

"What you saw was an Asfett. That is an Egyptian demon that can possess those who are corrupt of character. The thing is, only people who are descendants of an Egyptian god can see these demons. Are either of your parents' descendants of an Egyptian god?" he asked.

"Wait a minute! Egyptian gods, Egyptian demons, this is even crazier than when I thought aliens were possessing people!" shouted AJ defensively.

"I know it's hard to believe, Jamal." Said Terry, "But has either of your parents ever mentioned The Brotherhood of the All-Seeing Eye?" He proceeded to explain to Jamal about who AJ truly was and why demons were out to get him.

"Wait a minute, you expect me to believe that AJ is a reincarnated pharaoh and that thing that possessed the principal was an Egyptian demon?" asked Jamal, staring at Terry suspiciously.

"Do you have a better explanation for what you saw? If AJ had not been wearing the Eye of Horus, the Asfett would have killed you both. I know it's a lot to take in, but I don't have any reason toile to you, do I?" Said Terry.

"Okay, say I believe you, then what?" asked Jamal.

"Then we figure out how you fit into all of this." Terry responded.

"My mother never mentioned the Brotherhood of the All-Seeing Eye. My dad died before I was born, so I don't know anything about him," said Jamal.

"Can I have their names please? We have a database of BASE members, if either of your parents was ever a member, they'll be in the database." Said Terry.

"My dad's name was Paul Walker. My mom's name is Melissa Jenkins. She remarried after my dad died.

"I'm going back to my office to run your parents' names. I'll be in touch with you soon," said Terry.

CHAPTER 9

THE PROPHECY

Terry went back to his office and immediately logged into the Brotherhood of the All-Seeing Eye member database. First, he looked for Jamal's mom, Melissa. Melissa Jenkins name turned up nothing. But when he looked up Paul Walker's name That's when things got interesting.

Paul Walker had been a member of the Los Angeles chapter of BASE, according to his file he was a descendant of Heka, god of magic and healing. Terry knew that descendants of Heka are extremely rare, because Heka rarely took physical form. Heka was a very old and powerful god. He was not just the god of magic; he was magic personified. If magic could take a physical form, that form would be Heka. It was said that Heka had created Ra himself.

Reading Paul's profile, Terry learned that he died fighting the forces of Apep.

Apparently, there was a prophecy that a descendant of Heka would befriend the reincarnated pharaoh and help him fulfill his destiny. When Apep heard of this prophecy, he immediately dispatched some of his demons to kill Paul and his wife. Paul and several other BASE members died in the attack, but they saved his wife.

So, it was obviously no coincidence that Jamal had become friends with AJ. It had been foretold in a prophecy that he would befriend AJ. Terry needed to speak to Jamal's mother immediately. He called AJ and told him he needed Jamal's phone number. AJ gave it to him, and he called,

"Hello," said Jamal as he answered his phone.

"Hello Jamal, this is Terry, AJ's therapist. I need to speak to you and your mom immediately. I found out why you can see Egyptian demons. Is it okay, if I grab AJ and come over to your house and discuss this with you and your mom?"

"Why? What did you find out?" asked Jamal.

"It would be best if I talked about it with you and your mom in person." Terry replied.

"Okay, you can come over around 6:00, mom should be home from work by then."

"Great, I'll see you at 6:00 this evening," said Terry. He hung up and immediately called AJ to let him know that he would be picking him up at 6:00 that evening, to go to Jamal's house.

Later that evening, Terry and AJ met Jamal and his mother at their house. Divia and her father had gone out to see a movie, so they had the house to themselves. They were all sitting around the kitchen table, talking.

"I'm sorry to be so dramatic," started Terry, "Mrs. Jenkins, have you ever heard of the Brotherhood of the All-Seeing Eye also known as BASE?" Terry asked Jamal's mom.

"Please, call me Melissa," she paled as she began to answer the question, "My first husband, Paul, was a member of BASE before he died." She answered. "There was a prophecy about a descendant of Heka and demons attacked us. He died in the attack. That's why I moved here, to get away from all that. I realized I was pregnant with Jamal about a week after he died." All this came rushing out of her as if she had been holding it in for years. She blinked back tears.

"I'm sorry to have to tell you this, but you can't outrun a prophecy.

I'm a member of the local chapter of BASE. I read about the prophecy and it's fulfilling itself," said Terry.

"What are you talking about? That prophecy died with Paul! That's why the demon attacks stopped!" she said hysterically.

"What is this prophecy you guys keep talking about?" asked Jamal.

"I'd like to hear about it too," said AJ.

"Do you want to tell them or should I?" Terry asked Melissa.

"Jamal, before you were born, your father and I went to the carnival with your aunt and uncle. While we were there, we visited an old fortune teller. It was supposed to be for fun. When it was Paul's turn, she took his hand and her body went stiff and she seemed to go into some kind of trance. That's when she said the prophecy that would change our lives forever. She said that a descendant of Heka would help pharaoh fulfill his destiny and save the world. At that time, Paul was the only descendant of Heka that anyone knew of. Paul knew immediately that we were in danger. He told the other members about the prophecy and asked them to help protect us. The head of the chapter had us move into a house owned by BASE. He said it was more secure than our home. It was not only protected with physical security, but also with magical security. When the attack came, there were so many demons, and they were everywhere. Security did their best, but they were outnumbered. The magic spells placed on the house held out for a while, but soon we could tell the spells were weakening. That was when your father did the bravest thing I've ever seen in my life. He cast a protection spell so strong that it forced the demons to flee or be destroyed. A spell that strong has to be powered by some kind of sacrifice. Paul used his own life force to power it. He saved me, but gave up his own life in the process. I found out I was pregnant with you a week later. It never occurred to me that the prophecy might be about you." By the time she finished her story, Melissa was crying.

Jamal jumped up, ran to his mom and hugged her to comfort her. "Aw, mom don't cry, everything will be okay."

Melissa wiped the tears away wit. h her sleeve, "I'm sorry for being such a drama queen. It's just that I haven't thought about this in years. Such bad memories."

"Your husband sacrificed his life for you. He thought that with him dead, the prophecy would die with him, and the demon attacks would stop. And he was right. Until recently, there haven't been any attacks," said Terry.

"What do you mean, until recently?" Melissa asked hesitantly.

"AJ and Jamal were attacked by a demon at school yesterday. Fortunately, AJ was wearing the Eye of Horus and forced the demon to retreat. I had assumed the demon was after AJ, but it could have been after both of them." Said Terry.

"What are you talking about?" asked Melissa desperately.

"AJ is the pharaoh mentioned in the prophecy and it is Jamal's destiny to help him find his parents." Said Terry.

Melissa turned to face Jamal, "A demon attacked you and you didn't tell me? Why?" she asked him. Jamal, caught off guard, looked like a deer caught in headlights, took a deep breath, and said,

"First of all, I didn't know it was a demon. I thought it was an alien, and I thought you'd think I was crazy if I told you aliens were possessing people. Second, I didn't know about this prophecy. Why didn't you tell me about this before?" he asked her.

"Because after your father died, I thought the prophecy died with him. So did the rest of BASE. I was told that I would be safe because of Paul's sacrifice. You weren't even born yet." She said, starting to cry again. Terry cut in,

"Melissa, you didn't do anything wrong. You and everyone else thought the prophecy was about Paul. Your husband's sacrifice has protected you and Jamal all these years. But prophecies have a way of fulfilling themselves and these attacks are not going to stop until they fulfill their destinies."

At that point, the front door opened, and Divia and her father William came in. "Hey everybody, who wants chocolate chip ice cream? We picked up some on the way home from the movie." Asked Divia happily. AJ and Jamal were too stunned by what they were hearing to say anything, so Melissa said,

"Ice cream sounds nice right now. I think I'll have some."

"I think we could all use some ice cream right about now," agreed Terry. Both boys nodded numbly. Divia looked at Terry and said,

"Who are you?"

"My name is Terry. I'm a friend of AJ's. I've met your mom and your brother, but I don't know your name."

"I'm Divia and this is my dad, William," said Divia.

"Pleased to meet you both," said Terry, shaking their hands. William got some bowls and Divia scooped out the ice cream and gave everyone a bowl and then they handed out the bowls to everyone. Everyone at their bowl of ice cream in quiet contentment. Soon Terry said,

"It's been great meeting all of you, but I'm afraid it's time for me to go." And he left.

CHAPTER 10

THE DANCE

The next day after school, AJ was at Jamal's house playing basketball. Jamal left for a minute to go to the bathroom. Divia came outside and greeted him,

"Hey AJ, how's it going?" she asked.

"Pretty good. How about you Divia?" AJ replied. She approached him, "So arc you going to the school dance on Friday night?" she asked.

"No, are you?" AJ responded.

"No one has asked me yet," she said looking into his eyes and smiling. Fortunately, AJ took the hint.

"Hey Divia, do you want to go to the dance with me?" he asked her. She smiled at him and said,

"Well, since you asked so nicely, yes, I'd love to go to the dance with you."

"Great," AJ said awkwardly.

"Okay, I'll talk to you later," said Divia and went back into the house. AJ could not believe what had just happened. Not only was he going to the school dance, but he was also going with Divia! He wanted to dance and sing with joy. He was so excited, he forgot all about Jamal. Jamal came back from the bathroom, ready to play more basketball. But all AJ could think about was Divia and the dance.

"Where's your head at?" Jamal asked AJ, as a pass went right through his hands.

"Are you going to the dance on Friday?" AJ asked him.

"Yeah, with Kim," Jamal answered.

"Well, I'm going with Divia!" said AJ excitedly.

"At least she's going with someone I like. That fool Kyle asked her yesterday." Since hearing about the prophecy, AJ and Jamal hung around each other constantly. For protection, if nothing else. But soon, AJ decided to go home and talk to Angela.

"Hey Angela," said AJ as he walked into the house, "Guess what?" he asked her, trying to hold in his excitement.

"What?" asked Angela, smiling, sensing his excitement.

"I'm going to the dance with Divia!" he blurted out, unable to control his excitement any longer.

"That's great! Do you know how to dance?" she asked. Suddenly, all the excitement and joy he felt came rushing out of him, like air out of a balloon. How could he dance the night away with Divia, if he didn't know how to dance?

Angela saw the response her question got, and immediately tried to rectify the situation,

"Would you like me to teach you how to dance? She asked.

"Could you do that?" he asked excitedly.

"Of course I can. I taught Tim how to dance and I can teach you." Replied Angela. "But we need music and a place to dance. Help me move the sofa over to the wall so we have room to dance in the living room." They both pushed the sofa, until it was against the far wall.

"Now let me explain how most school dances go. When you first get there, your date will go to the bathroom with her friends. You'll wait for her to come back with Jamal. In a few minutes, your dates will come back. The DJ will be playing music, but no one will get on the dance floor until the first slow song comes on. That's when everybody gets on the floor to dance. So, I guess the first thing I should teach you is how to slow dance. Okay, slow dancing is like a long hug, and you sway to the music. Now come here." She played a slow song on her phone. "Put your hands on my back and I'll put my arms around your neck and then you just sway back and forth to the music." They started dancing.

"Very good AJ," said Angela, "You slow dance very well, now let's try regular dancing." She changed the music on her phone from a slow song to a fast one. She started dancing, but AJ just looked at her like she was crazy. "I told you, I don't know how to dance," he said.

"Okay, let's start with a simple dance called the two-step. Now watch my feet, and one and two, and one and two," AJ copied her moves.

"Good, now loosen up some, dancing is supposed to be fun. Think happy thoughts," Angela said jokingly. AJ thought about how great it would be dancing with Divia and soon he was dancing happily with Angela across the living room floor.

It was the night of the big dance and AJ was pacing around his room nervously. Angela poked her head into his room.

"Calm down AJ," she said, "You look great, you dance great, everything is going to be fine. Now come sit down, so I can braid your hair." AJ came out of his room and sat down in front of her. After a while, she had his hair braided into neat horizontal rows. As soon as she finished, he went to the bathroom to look in the mirror. He couldn't believe who looked back at him. The corn rows completely changed his look. He looked cool for once. With his braided hair, his shirt and tie and slim build, he could have been one of the cool kids at school.

"The corn rows look great, thank you Angela!" he yelled after admiring himself in the mirror.

Meanwhile, at Divia and Jamal's house, "I hate my hair!" Divia shouted from her room.

"I'm coming," shouted her mother as she raced from the kitchen to Divia's bedroom. "Okay, what's wrong with your hair?" Melissa asked as she reached her room.

"Well, I wanted to show off my natural curls, but it's just so frizzy," complained Divia, "AJ is going to be embarrassed to be seen with me."

"Honey, I think you could show up bald, and AJ would be proud to be your date," said her mother. At this point, Jamal interrupted and said, "Oh mom, I'm bald, do you think AJ will be ashamed to be seen with me?" in an impersonation of Divia's voice.

"Jamal, stop teasing your sister. Divia, come with me into my bathroom. I think I have something for your hair." Jamal went into his room laughing and Divia followed her mother into the bathroom. Melissa squirted some relaxer into her hand and began to work it into her daughter's hair. She waited a few minutes and then began to comb her hair.

"But mom, now my hair is straight like it normally is, I wanted curls," said Divia.

"Oh honey, I'm not done yet," said her mom. She got a can of hairspray and her curling iron and went to work. Soon Divia had long curls that framed her face and came down to her shoulders.

"Oh mom, it's perfect. Thank you so much," Squealed Divia.

"You're welcome, dear," replied her mom, "Now put on your dancing shoes and let's go to that dance! Jamal, that means you too! We leave for the dance in five minutes!"

They arrived at the dance the same time AJ and Angela did. "I'll pick you up here10:00" Said Angela said as AJ got out of the car. He was walking towards Jamal and Divia's car when Divia got out and he caught his breath. She looked beautiful. She wore a strapless, black dress that showed off her slim figure. Her hair was in long curls that framed her face and came down to her shoulders. As far as AJ was concerned, she was the most beautiful girl in the world.

"Wow! "You look great," was all he could manage to say.

"Thank you, you're not so bad yourself. I love the braids," she replied. Jamal got out of the car and said,

"If you two love birds will excuse me for a moment, I think that's my date pulling up over there." He walked over to a car pulling up into the parking lot. He returned a moment later with Kim Freeman on his arm. The girls began talking to each other and this AJ and Jamal a chance to talk. Jamal said,

"Hey man, you look good. The braids turned out nice."

"Thanks man, you look good too. I like your shirt and tie. Replied AJ. Jamal looked at AJ nervously and said,

"Are you wearing the Eye of Horus, just in case anything weird happens tonight?"

"To be honest, I never take off the Eye of Horus. The girls are wrapping up, we'd better get back to our dates. They went back to the girls and walked into the dance. Strobe lights lit up the auditorium as music blasted out of it. The music was great, but just as Angela had predicted, no one was dancing. Then a slow song came on, and a few couples including AJ and Divia ventured onto the dance floor. AJ was so thrilled to have Divia in his arms, he almost forgot how to dance. But as soon as he started moving, it all came back to him. He inhaled the smell of her perfume, intoxicated. He held her by the small of her back swaying back and forth with her. She looked into his eyes, and he couldn't help himself. He kissed her. To his surprise she kissed him back and deepened the kiss. The slow song ended, and everyone began to fast dance. After a few songs, Divia said she had to go to the bathroom and would be right back. He looked for Jamal, but he was still dancing with Kim. So he stood on the side by himself, happily thinking about Divia.

That's when Heidi Anderson approached him. Heidi was a stuck up white girl who had never said a word to him before.

"Hey AJ, you're looking good, do you want to dance?" she asked him.

"Um, no thanks. I'm here with Divia," AJ answered nervously, wondering why she was even talking to him.

"Oh come on AJ, if Divia didn't want you dancing with other girls, she shouldn't have left you here all alone," said Heidi as she began dancing with him. He just stared at her and did not dance with her. Heidi swayed her hips seductively and said, "Come on AJ, don't you want to dance with me? AJ definitely did not want to dance with Heidi, but there was something about the way she moved her hips and her voice that seemed to put him in a trance. He was about to give in and dance with her, when Divia returned. She got into Heidi's face and yelled,

"Heidi Anderson! Why are you trying to dance with my man?" Divia's voice broke the trance Heidi had AJ in. Heidi turned to Divia and hissed at her in a snakelike voice,

"You bitch! I almost had him!" Then dropping all pretenses of humanity, her skin paled, she sprouted giant bat-like wings from her back, and horns grew out of the sides of her head.

"This is not over Alexander Washington, for you or your friends. " We know who you are!" she said ominously and disappeared in a cloud of smoke. Jamal walked over to AJ and said,

"Is it just me, or is everyone at this school a demon in disguise?" AJ ignored Jamal and focused on Divia.

"Are you okay? Did she hurt you?" He asked her. She looked at him like he was crazy and said,

"Heidi Anderson, hurt me? Please, you saw how she ran away when I called her out." As if nothing strange had just happened. It occurred to AJ that she hadn't seen the demon because she was not descended from an Egyptian god. Unbeknownst to AJ, Divia had seen the demon. But if she told him that, it would lead to a lot of questions she did not want to answer. The dance ended and AJ and Divia went outside. They kissed one last time as her father, William pulled up. She ended the kiss with a hasty goodbye, afraid her father might get out of the car and strangle AJ.

AJ was on top of the world. He, Alexander James Washington, was dating Divia. Even a demon attack couldn't ruin this night, he was so happy. When Angela pulled up to pick him up, he couldn't stop smiling.

"Looks like someone had a good time at the dance," commented Angela, smiling at AJ.

"Yeah, it was great," replied AJ. They drove the rest of the way home in silence.

The next day, AJ called Terry to tell him about the demon attack at the dance. He explained how the demon tried to make him dance with her and how much he wanted to, until he heard Divia's voice.

"Sounds like a siren. Their voices have been known to hypnotize men. Men have been known to kill themselNves because a Siren told them to. Also sounds like she was trying to lure you into the dance of death." Said Terry.

"What's the Dance of Death?" asked AJ.

"It's a dance where the Siren kills you as you are dancing with her. No mortal has ever survived the Dance of Death. Divia must have a very powerful voice, to pull you out of the trance the Siren had you in." Terry noted.

The week passed like a blur. At first AJ tried to divide his time Jamal and Divia. Then he started spending all his time with Divia. He loved being with her. He loved everything about her; the way she walked, the way she talked, the way she smelled and especially the way she kissed.

As much as he loved being with Divia, he was worried that being with her might put her in danger. After all, a demon did attack him on their first date. That night the demon had just disappeared in a puff of smoke, but what if the Siren had hurt Divia? AJ didn't think he could live with himself if she got hurt because of him. He never knew when the next demon attack was coming, but he always knew one was coming. After a couple of weeks of being worried sick that something might happen to her, AJ decided to tell her the truth. One day, while AJ was at Divia and Jamal's house, he asked her,

"Divia, can we go for a walk?"

"Sure, just let me put on my shoes," she replied as she got up off the couch.

"So, what's up babe?" she asked as they walked out the door.

"Let me start by saying this past month with you has been the best time of my life," he started, when she interrupted.

"Wait, are you trying to break up with me?" she asked accusingly.

"Me, break up with you? Never!"

She took a deep breath, "Okay then, what did you want to say?"

"I'm trying to tell you the truth about who I am," he said.

"What are you talking about AJ?" Divia asked.

"This is going to sound weird and hard to believe, and if you decide that I'm just crazy and never want to see me again. I'll understand," said AJ.

"I still don't know what you're talking about AJ" said Divia.

"In a nutshell, I'm a reincarnated pharaoh. I've got to fulfill my destiny and demons are constantly attacking me and those around me. And I really don't want you to get hurt because of me." AJ blurted out. She handled it better than he thought she would, she laughed.

"This is a joke, right?" she said.

"I wish it was a joke. But I'm dead serious. And just so you know, I'm not the only one who believes it, so does Jamal and so does your mom." Said AJ

"Wait a minute. You told Jamal and my mom about this, before you told me?" asked Divia.

"Actually, we all kind of found out together," said AJ. Divia thought about it for a moment, steeled herself and said,

"Whatever demons come after you will have o get through me." AJ was surprised by how confident she sounded. He felt relieved to have told Divia the truth and he was happy she was handling it so well. He walked over to her, held her hand and kissed her.

"Thank you for being you," he said to her and kissed her.

CHAPTER 11

CASTING A MAGIC SPELL

The next morning, AJ got a call from Terry.

"Hey Terry," said AJ as he answered his phone.

"Hello AJ, I have some good news. I think I may have found a way to find your parents," said Terry excitedly.

"Really?" said AJ, his eyes growing wide with excitement, "How?"

"It involves both you and Jamal, so I should probably tell you both at the same time. Could I meet with the two of you at your house later today?" he asked.

"I'll ask Jamal to come over after school today," said AJ.

In the cafeteria at lunchtime, AJ spoke with Jamal.

"Hey man, do you think you could come over to my house after school today? Terry wants to talk to us." AJ said to Jamal.

"Sure, I'll be there. What does he want to talk about?"

"He thinks he might have found a way to find my parents, but it involves both of us, so he wanted to talk to us at the same time." AJ called Terry to let him know that he and Jamal would be at his house after school. Terry arrived at AJ's house and began to explain his plan.

"I've been searching through the BASE archives, trying to find something that will help find your parents, and I think I may have found something. I found a magic spell for finding lost things. It's basically a prayer to Shai, the god of fate and fortune. Jamal, because you're a descendant of Heka, god of magic, any spell we cast will be super-charged."

"But I don't know anything about magic," protested Jamal.

"It doesn't matter, the magic is in your blood." Replied Terry, "Now AJ do you remember when I made you practice writing hieroglyphics?"

"Yes," replied AJ.

"Good, you need to write the hieroglyphics for magic, Shai, and ancestor on this piece of paper," Said Terry, handing him a piece of paper. "Good, now Jamal, I need you to say out loud," I Jamal Walker, call upon my ancestor, Heka to aid me with this magic spell." Both boys did as they were told. AJ wasn't sure what to expect, maybe sudden knowledge of where his parents were, or maybe some thunder. Instead, nothing happened, absolutely nothing.

"Did anything happen?" AJ asked out loud.

"I certainly didn't feel anything," said Jamal.

"Relax," said Terry, "magic spells like this can take a little time to work." The rest of the day went by without any hint that the magic spell had worked. That night, as AJ prepared for bed, he had a discussion with Bastet.

"Bastet?" he called to her in his dark bedroom. A voice responded in his head,

"I am here."

"Terry, Jamal and I cast a magic spell to find my parents earlier today," he told her.

"And how did that go?" asked Bastet mid-yawn.

"Well, nothing happened, but Terry says it can take some time for the spell to work," replied AJ.

"He is correct. Which god was the spell directed to?" she asked.

"Shai, god of fate and fortune."

"Shai is an elusive god, he will answer your prayer, but it might not be in the way you expect," Bastet warned.

CHAPTER 12

THE FORTUNE COOKIE

Two weeks passed, with no results from the magic spell. AJ and Divia were having Chinese food for lunch. As they finished their meal, AJ reached into the bag to get their fortune cookies. The first thing they noticed was that both of their fortune cookies were chocolate.

"Cool," they both said. AJ opened his fortune cookie and it said, "Find the lost god. Your lucky numbers are 21,25,46,17,80." AJ did not know what to make of this. He had never opened a fortune cookie and got a fortune like this before. He asked Divia what hers said.

"Good fortune is heading your way," she responded, " What does yours say?"

"It says to find the lost god, whatever that means." They finished their meal and they both went home. Later that evening, AJ was in his room,

" Bastet?"

"I am here," she responded mentally.

"I got a weird fortune cookie today. It said to find the lost god and then it gave me my lucky numbers. Do you have any idea what this means?" he asked her.

"It means your spell worked," replied Bastet and she laughed, "The god of fortune, communicating through a fortune cookie. Oh, I love the irony."

"What do you mean the spell worked? I still don't know where my parents are." Said AJ.

"Ah, but you have received your first clue on how to find them," said Bastet, "You must find the lost god."

"But who is the lost god and how do I find him?" asked AJ desperately.

"The lost god is Maat, god of justice. As to how to find her, you should probably ask Osiris." Said Bastet.

"Osiris, as in the god of the dead? How am I supposed to see him?" he asked.

"As I told you before, you are pharaoh, Egypt is within you," she replied.

"The last time you said that you took me to Egypt to see the Sphinx. Are you going to take me to the underworld this time?" AJ asked.

"Do you know of a better way to get to the underworld?" asked Bastet in response.

"I guess not, when do we leave?"

"Tonight, when you fall asleep. I can control your dream and take you to the underworld." AJ thought that he would never be able to fall asleep, wondering what the underworld would be like. But sleep came for him sooner than he thought it would. As he fell asleep, he immediately began to dream. The next thing he knew, he was in a throne room. At the other end of the throne room, a good looking, muscular, bald, black man sat on a throne. Standing next to him, was the Jackal headed god, Anubis, god of embalming. Bastet was next to him in human form. They approached the gods. So much power emanated from the two gods, that the hair on AJ's arms stood on end. The gods were so engrossed in their conversation that they did not notice AJ or Bastet. Bastet interrupted their conversation with a polite, "Excuse me my lord." Both gods looked surprised to have company. Osiris said,

"Ah Bastet, it has been too long. And who is this you bring with you? It is rare that the living come to the underworld, to what do I owe the pleasure?"

AJ said, "Lord Osiris, my name is Alexander Washington, and I'm the reincarnation of pharaoh Ramses."

Osiris laughed and said, "Are you? Well, how can I help you Ramses?"

AJ swallowed and said, "The god Shai sent me a message in a fortune cookie. It said to free the lost god. Bastet said that Maat is the lost god and that you might know where she is. Do you know where the lost god Maat is?" He showed Osiris the fortune from his fortune cookie.

"Ah Shair, up to his usual tricks. Maat was lost when what she represented; Justice, balance and control, stopped being valued in the upperworld. She was tricked and taken by the forces of Apep. She has been lost for a long time. You will need these two things to free her." He gave AJ an ostrich feather and a golden ankh. "The ostrich feather is her symbol, and the ankh is carried by all Egyptian gods. She is in room 134."

"Wait, room 134? What does that mean? Where is she being held?" AJ asked desperately.

"Shai already told you. It's on your fortune," said Osiris and with a wave of his hand AJ was back in his, his audience with Osiris was over. AJ woke up and immediately said,

"Bastet, are you there?"

"I am right here," her voice spoke in his mind.

"What did Osiris mean when he said that Maat was in room 134?" he asked her.

"I do not know. Perhaps you and your friends can figure it out," she replied. Later that day, AJ was with Divia, Jamal, Terry and Angela. He had told them about his trip to the underworld and what Osiris had said. They were discussing it over pizza at Angela's house.

"We've looked at the fortune a thousand times. It says, "Free the lost god". We know that Maat is the lost god, but the fortune doesn't tell us where she is or how to free her. This is so frustrating." Said Angela. "Can I see your fortune again AJ?" He handed it to her. "Let's look at these lucky numbers again, 21,25,46,17.80. It looks like 5 lucky numbers, but grouped differently, (212)546-1780 you get a phone number. Maybe you're supposed to call the phone number?"

""That's brilliant Angela! I can't believe I missed it!" exclaimed Terry. They all agreed that this must be the answer. So, AJ called the phone number.

"Thank you for calling Golden Oaks Senior Center. How may I direct your call?" Said the operator.

"Um, can you connect to room 134, please?" asked AJ.

"I'm sorry, room 134 is not available at this time. Can I help you with something else?" Said the operator politely.

"Yes, where are you located?"

"We are located at 2358 17th Street."

"Thank you very much," said AJ and hung up, "Okay," he told the others, "it's a senior citizen's center. I tried to get room 134, but it was unavailable. It's located at 2358

17th Street. So, I guess we know where Maat is being kept. Now we just have to figure out how to free her."

"Well, we can't just walk in and go Where's Maat, we're taking her with us." Said Terry, "If that's where they're holding her, there will be demonic guards everywhere. Not to mention magical security."

"We shouldn't just go in there without knowing the layout of the place and where Maat is," said Jamal, "We need to send in a spy."

"I have a suggestion," said Angela, "What if AJ, Divia, and Jamal said they wanted to volunteer at the senior citizen center for extra credit at school? Senior citizens love it when young people come by to chat with them."

"Another great idea, Angela," said Terry, "I'll call Golden Oaks Senior Center and tell them that I'm the school counselor and I have 3 students who need extra credit, and would it be possible for them to volunteer there."

Terry took out his phone and called The Golden Oaks Senior Center.

"Golden Oaks Senior Center, how may I direct your call?" asked the same operator who had spoken to AJ.

"Yes, my name is Dr. Terrence Conners, counselor at Harriet Dubois Middle School. I was wondering if you have any volunteer opportunities for some of my students who need extra credit?" he asked.

"You would need to talk to the administrator about that, please hold." Said the operator.

"This is Dr. Atkins, how can I help you?" said a female voice into the phone.

"Hello Dr. Atkins, this is Dr. Terrance Conners of Harriet Dubois Middle School. I was wondering if you need any volunteers?" asked Terry.

"We can always use volunteers," said Dr. Atkins excitedly, "how many?"

"Three, I was thinking that maybe they could volunteer after school for a couple of hours for a month, maybe?" Terry asked tentatively.

"Sounds great," said Dr. Atkins.

"Alright, thank you very much for your help. They'll report for duty, first thing after school on Monday. If you have any questions, please feel free to to call my office at (212)555-8842." Said Terry and hung up the phone. "Okay, I got you kids lined up volunteer jobs at the senior center."

"Let me make sure I've got this right," said AJ, "I, a reincarnated pharaoh, am supposed to walk into a building full of demons that probably want to kill me, with my best friend and my girlfriend, scout the place out, without setting off any alarms or anyone noticing? This has got to be the worst plan in history! And you're going to get all three of us killed!"

"I almost forgot the most important part of the plan. If you get into any trouble, you just push the number 9 on your phone and all thelocal members of BASE will come rushing in to rescue you." Said Terry.

"I have a better idea, Bastet and I will go in and look around. When we trip off some alarm or someone gets suspicious, as they inevitably will. Baste will only have me to protect."

"But why should you go?" asked Angela, "Why not me or Terry or some other member of BASE?"

"Because Bastet only talks to me," answered AJ, "And having a god on my side greatly increases my chances of survival." They all agreed that this was the best course of action. Although Divia and Angela did not like the idea of AJ going in all by himself.

CHAPTER 13

THE SENIOR CITIZEN'S CENTER

Sunday evening, AJ spoke with Bastet, "Bastet?"

"I am here," she responded.

"I took it for granted that you would come with me tomorrow. Will you come with me to free Maat tomorrow?"

"Of course I will. I'm here to help you fulfill your destiny," said Bastet, "Besides, I think you're going to need my other half."

"Up to this point, you have only dealt with me as Bastet. But long ago, Egyptians began to think of me and her as one deity, so we merged into one." Said Bastet.

"Who are you talking about?" asked AJ.

"Sekhmet, goddess of war. She's kind of like me after 10 espressos. I call her angry me. If you are going into a building full of demons, you'll probably need her at some point." Said Bastet.

Monday finally came and AJ put Bastet in his backpack and headed to Golden Oaks Senior Center. He left his backpack partially unzipped, so Bastet could see out. When he arrived there, a security guard was sitting at a desk in the front of the facility.

"Hi, my name is AJ Washington. I'm from Harriet Dubois Middle School and I'm supposed to start volunteering today." Said AJ. The security guard looked up and said,

"You'll need to check in with Dr. Atkins. First door on your right," he said as he pointed in the direction that AJ needed to go. AJ walked in the direction the security guard had pointed and came to a door that said Dr. D. Atkins Administrator on it. Bastet's voice spoke to his mind.

"The security guard is a demon in disguise, this place reeks of demons," she said.

"Well, for right now they're putting up a good front. Like everything is business as usual. So, let's not start any trouble until we have to. He knocked on the administrator's door.

"Come in," said a female voice. AJ opened the door and walked in. A secretary sat behind a desk facing AJ as he walked in. He went up to her and said,

"Hi, I'm Alexander Washington. I'm from Harriet Dubois Middle School and I'm supposed to start volunteering here today."

"Oh yes, the doctor is expecting you, go right in and see her." Said the secretary.

From the moment he walked into the administrator's office, AJ knew something was wrong. First, the Eye of Horus immediately started growing warm against his chest. Second, Bastet said,

"Be careful, she is not human at all." There was nothing overtly wrong with Dr. Atkins, in fact she seemed very friendly. She was a stout, middle aged white woman, with short blonde hair.

"Hello, you must be the student from Dubois Middle School. My name is Dr. Atkins. How are you today?"

"I'm fine, thank you. My name is Alexander Washington. How can I help out here today?" asked AJ.

"Oh, I think we'll start you in the kitchen, helping to prepare meals. My secretary, Charlene will take you to the kitchen and the workers there will show you what to do." The secretary from the front gave AJ a tour of the place as she took him to the kitchen.

"And over there is the recreation room. We have a ping pong table and a TV in there, but the residents mostly like to read the paper and drink coffee in there." She commented as they walked by what was the recreation room.

"And where do the residents stay?" asked AJ.

"They have rooms down that hallway," she said as they passed a hallway. "But today, you're going to the kitchen, which is right here." They arrived at the kitchen and the cafeteria. "Hey Tom," she said to one of the people working in the kitchen, "this is the volunteer from the middle school. Give him something to do."

"Hey little man, what brings you to this hellhole?" he asked AJ.

"I need more credits at school, so I'm volunteering here to get them," said AJ.

"You can start by bringing these trays of food out to the clients in the cafeteria for lunch. AJ began to bring trays of food out to the clients. He talked to them as he delivered their food.

"What's your name?" asked one woman as he gave her a tray of food.

"My name is Alexander. What's your name?" responded AJ.

"My name is Gladys," said the old woman, "You remind me of my grandson. He's handsome too, like you.

"Thank you ma'am," said AJ.

"Oh dear, I seem to have left my glasses in my room. Could you be a dear and get them for me Alexander?" she asked.

"Yes ma'am, which room do you stay in?" he asked her.

"Room 136. My glasses should be on the chair next to the window," Said Gladys.

"I'll be right back with your glasses," said AJ. He and Bastet walked back to the hallway they had walked by earlier and began looking at the numbers on the doors. They walked past room 134 on the way to Gladys's room and Bastet noted. "Room 134 is protected by ancient magic. There are also guards behind the door." AJ tried the doorknob, but it was locked.

"Well, room 134 is obviously where there holding Maat, but we already knew that. Now the question is how do we get in there and save her, without getting killed by security or the ancient magic?"

"How do we get in?" asked Bastet, obviously offended. "I am a god am I not? I go where I please, ancient magic or not!"

"Okay, so how do we get in again?" AJ asked.

"Just knock on the door. The guards are low level demons, like the ones that came out of your closet. The Eye should take care of them. I can get us past the magical barrier." Said Bastet.

CHAPTER 14

THE BATTLE FOR MAAT

AJ went to room 134 and knocked on the door as Bastet had suggested he do. A guard opened the door and said gruffly, "What do you want?"

"Gladys has lost her glasses and thinks they might be in here. Do you mind if I look for them?" asked AJ. The guard looked confused. (low level demons are not known for their intelligence) AJ pushed his way in past the guard and showed him and his partner the Eye of Horus and they immediately burned into piles of ashes. He walked into the room with Bastet at his side. He knew when they breached the magical barrier because an alarm went off. AJ had not been sure what Maat would look like, but he sure wasn't prepared for what he saw. An elderly woman in a wheelchair with an oxygen mask over her face sat in front of him.

"Are you Maat?" he asked.

"No, I'm Florence, now go away and leave me alone!" she said in a crabby, old person voice. AJ looked at Bastet and said,

"What do I do now?"

"She has been imprisoned in this body so long she has forgotten who she is. Give her the symbols Osiris gave to you" she said. First, AJ took the feather out of his backpack. He showed it to her and said,

"Do you remember this? It is your symbol. You weighed the hearts of men against it to determine where to send them after they died." He then reached into his backpack and pulled out the Ankh that Osiris had given him. "And this, all Egyptian gods carry an ankh. You are not Florence. You are the goddess Maat. God of truth, justice and control, and humankind needs you back." He laid the objects on her lap. There was a blinding light and a sound like thunder and there stood Maat, in all her glory. No longer an old woman in a wheelchair, but now a young African woman with wings on her arms.

"I'M FREE!" she shouted. Bastet said, "More guards are coming and so is the administrator. I will leave now because you need her."

"Wait a minute!" shouted AJ, "What do you mean you're leaving now?!?" Bastet, who was in the form of a cat morphed back into human form. But she did not look like she normally did when she took human form. In fact, this was not Bastet at all. She looked just as beautiful as Bastet, but in a different way. Whereas Bastet had long, beautiful hair, this woman was bald. She was tall and muscular, like a warrior. Her muscles were taut, like a lion about to spring on its prey. And she was looking at AAJ like he might be that prey. So, AJ nervously said,

"Hi, I'm AJ and you are?"

"I am Sekhmet, goddess of battle," she replied in a booming voice. "No pharaoh goes to battle without me at his side." As if on cue, security showed up. There were dozens of demons everywhere, and in the middle of them all stood the administrator, Dr. Atkins, still in her pants suit.

"TO BATTLE!" yelled Sekhmet and transformed into a lioness and rushed the demons. She roared at the demons and the sound made them all disintegrate, all except Dr. Atkins.

"It will take more than your bad breath to defeat me!" She yelled at Sekhmet. And then she began to change into her true form. Her body morphed until she was 10 feet tall with red skin, and goat hooves for feet. AJ thought she looked like the devil himself, but he decided he shouldn't say anything because at the moment, he was so scared, he was doing his best not to wet his pants.

Sekhmet was obviously not afraid of the demon and seemed to know him by name. "Ah, Bazul, we meet in battle again," she said.

Dr. Atkins/Bazul said,

"Sekhmet! My powers have grown since we last fought," he glanced at AJ, "And don't think I've forgotten about you, boy!" He winked his left eye and a bolt of lightning shot out of nowhere and hit AJ in the chest. He would have died, but the Eye of Horus absorbed the lightning and shot it back out at the monster. The monster was surprised, but unharmed.

"The boy is protected by the Eye of Horus! You cannot harm him, you fool!" yelled Sekhmet. She was now as tall as he was and was carrying a spear and a shield.

"I've grown more powerful over time. You are no longer powerful enough to defeat me by yourself." Said Bazul.

"Bazul, lord of lies. I am not here alone. The goddess of truth is here with me, and she has a bone to pick with you." And standing there, no longer a frail, old woman, but a beautiful, goddess was Maat, goddess of truth and justice.

"For decades, you have held me here against my will, stripped of my powers. But rest assured, I have all my power back now. So, lord of lies, feel my Flames of Truth!" And with that she pointed her widespread hands at him and shouted, "Enflamare!" Suddenly, Bazul was engulfed in blue flames. He screamed in agony as the flames grew hotter. The flames emitted so much heat they disintegrated Bazul and made AJ pass out.

CHAPTER 15

THE TATTOO

When AJ woke up, he was laying on his bed, surrounded by friends. As soon as he opened his eyes, Divia squealed, "Look, he's waking up!" Everyone in the room turned to look at him.

"What happened? How did I get here?" asked AJ. Terry, who was standing at the foot of his bed said,

"I believe I can answer your questions AJ. First of all, you did it, you freed the lost god. As to how you got here, Bastet brought you here and explained what happened."

"Where is Bastet? She left and some god named Sekhmet showed up and fought all the demons." Said AJ sounding like he was crazy. Bastet walked into the room in human form. She spoke out loud, so everyone could hear her.

"Let me explain AJ. Long ago, Sekhmet and I became one god. It's kind of like we're gods living in the same body. I had to leave so she could come and help you."

"I have another question," said AJ. "If Osiris knew where Maat was, why didn't he just rescue her a long time ago?"

"Osiris is a god of the underworld. He cannot leave the underworld or chaos would ensue. Besides that, humankind needed to want Maat back and all she represents. Your rescuing her, proved that humanity wanted her back." Said Bastet. "By the way, Maat would like a word with you." Bastet shimmered and disappeared, and, in her place, another African woman appeared. She was just as beautiful as Bastet, but she was taller and darker skinned. She also had feathers running down her arms like wings.

"Alexander Washington, my savior, thank you so much for rescuing me," said Maat.

"Um, you're welcome, but I didn't really do anything, Sekhmet did. All I did was pass out," AJ admitted.

"You are humble. But you did much more than pass out You were the one who freed me from my prison. My prison was not the Senior Center, it was the body they had me trapped in and you freed me with my feather and my ankh." As AJ sat up in bed, he noticed a mark on his arm that looked a lot like the Eye of Horus. He asked Maat about it.

"Excuse me M. Maat, but do you know where this came from?" he asked, showing her the mark on his arm. She nodded and said,

"All pharaohs have three tattoos. One that proves they are protected by the gods. One that shows they honor the gods and one that shows the divine right to rule. That is your first tattoo, it shows that you are protected by the gods. They are magical tattoos, that must be earned, that's why it just showed up on your body. When you have earned all three tattoos you will be ready to fulfill your destiny." She answered.

"Great, I've got to earn more of these things. I'm guessing that means fighting more demons." Said AJ, in a tired voice. Jamal walked over to his bed and said,

"Hey man, no matter what comes up, I'll be right there, by your side. We're destined to be best friends, man." He put his hand on AJ's shoulder. Then, Divia got up and said,

"I already told you, any demons that come after you, will have to go through me, and I meant it." She walked over to his bed and gave him a kiss. "I got your back, babe." She whispered in his ear.

AJ couldn't help but worry about what the future might hold. But he was glad he was not facing the future alone. Whatever adventures came, he had Jamal, Divia and the members of BASE on his side. This put a smile on his face.

www.ingramcontent.com/pod-product-compliance
Lightning Source LLC
Chambersburg PA
CBHW020735310726
48969CB00003B/844